Sherlock Holmes at Oxford

Nicholas Utechin

Second Edition

RD

Robert Dugdale
Oxford

First published in 1977 by Robert Dugdale,
c/o Corpus Christi College, OXFORD, OX1 4JF

First Edition June 1977
Reprinted October 1977
Second edition 1981
Reprinted 1985

British Library Cataloguing in Publication Data
Utechin, Nicholas
Sherlock Holmes at Oxford. - 2nd ed.
1. Doyle, *Sir* Arthur Conan - Characters - Sherlock Holmes
2. Universities and colleges in literature
I. Title
823'. 912 PR4624

ISBN 0-9503880-8-4

Cover design by Paul Clark

Set in 11/12 pt Baskerville and
printed in Great Britain by
Parchment (Oxford) Ltd, 60 Hurst Street,
OXFORD, OX4 1HD

Contents

Note to the 1985 Impression

For this impression the postscript has been updated, and a few further corrections have been made.

Oxford, 14 September 1985 N.R.U.

Note to the Second Edition

For this new edition a postscript and bibliography have been added, a few minor corrections have been made, and the cover has been redesigned.

Acknowledgements

I am indebted to William Beaver, who unearthed the picture of Holmes as an undergraduate on the cover, and to Dr Julian Wolff of New York, Editor of *The Baker Street Journal*, for allowing me to use an article of mine from that journal as the basis for the section entitled 'The College'. I should also like to thank the Oxford City Library for permission to reproduce the photographs, and C. E. Braybrooke of the Bodleian Library, Oxford, for photographing the cover illustration of Holmes (from *The Graphic,* 1882). I should like to express special thanks to my publisher, Robert Dugdale, who has backed my confidence in this project with his expertise and enthusiasm.

Introduction

Those for whom the name 'Sherlock Holmes' has a mysterious attraction and fascination will need no explanation for the publication of this slim volume: they will know already that the question of the Great Man's university has long been a source of scholarly argument on both sides of the Atlantic in such erudite periodicals as *The Sherlock Holmes Journal* and *The Baker Street Journal*. Those of you, on the other hand, to whom the name conjures up the slavering Baskerville Hound, the face of Basil Rathbone and little more, may need — nay, have a right to expect — a short word of clarification.

There is, I think, an unassailable argument in favour of Sherlock Holmes being the most famous and best-loved character in all fiction. Most people, of course, know that in reality he is nothing more than the creation of Sir Arthur Conan Doyle's imagination (although letters still arrive in Baker Street addressed to the detective himself). But while there are Dickens Societies and Brontë Fellowships, nowhere is there a Conan Doyle Coterie — on the contrary, there are literally dozens of Sherlock Holmes societies throughout the world, devoted to 'keeping the memory green'. And have no doubts on this score: there is enough material in the sixty stories to feed the extraordinary amount of pseudo-scholarship that appears as each year passes — the chronological problems, the number of Dr Watson's wives, the exact location of the good doctor's wound (the shoulder? the leg? even the buttock has been suggested!), the true identity of that Napoleon of Crime, Professor Moriarty . . . and the choice of Oxford or Cambridge as Holmes's university back in the 1870s.

In one sense, it's all a game, of course, and yet a game, as Dorothy L. Sayers once said, that should be played 'as seriously as a county cricket match at Lord's'; and it is therefore in this spirit of fun, of playing an intriguing game, that we can embark on an identification, with proof to back up the assertion, of Oxford as the place of learning that moulded the young (*very* young, as I shall suggest later) Sherlock Holmes into the greatest detective the pages of fiction and the world have ever known. I do not apologise for the fact that I approached the question with my mind less than completely open: it does not take much for an Oxford man to choose his own birthplace and university over the rival claims of Cambridge — but then, the evidence is there! It must be mentioned that strange, sad cases have been made on behalf of King's College, London, Queen's College, Birmingham and Owens College, Manchester — with passing sorrow but never a backward glance, let us consign the proponents of such outrageous theories to some shadowy critics' graveyard.

The basic source material, of course, must be the printed words in the Sherlock Holmes Canon, and quotations from it appear throughout this booklet; other evidence adduced one way or the other by the many eminent writers who have contributed to the literature comes from their own researches, as will soon become apparent when you follow the twisting and turning strands of argument.

Oxford . . . or Cambridge?

The laurel for the most famous dog in the Sherlock Holmes Canon must surely be awarded to that most negative of canines, the dog that did nothing in the night-time — while all round was occurring the most nefarious mayhem — during the case chronicled by Dr Watson as *Silver Blaze*. He wins, however, by no more than a muzzle: closely contesting the honour will inevitably be the terrifying, phosphor-coated Hound of the Baskervilles. But spare a thought for a small bull-terrier which, in 1871, 'froze' on to Holmes's ankle. That little pup has been a subject more disputed by scholars in the Sherlockian world than any other — animal, vegetable or mineral. The ink spent on discussing the locale of those snapping jaws would serve to drown even the burly figure of Watson's agent (or so the legend goes), one Arthur Conan Doyle. Why the locale, you ask? Wherein lies its significance? Certainly the dog deserves its reputation, for, as a result of the incident, the undergraduate Sherlock Holmes met its owner, Victor Trevor, and soon thereafter embarked upon the first case in which he could put to use his unique powers. But the overriding question remains: did those jaws come down on that ankle in Oxford or Cambridge?

That terrier, you see, plays a central role on the stage of controversy surrounding Holmes's undergraduate days. Which of the two great universities can claim Sherlock as its own? The title of this booklet gives away my own ideas on the subject, but we shall, of course, give a fair crack of the whip to protagonists of the other camp and work through the evidence, letting it speak for itself. Enter, then, the curious incident of the dog in the morning.

The exact quotation may be found in *The Gloria Scott*. Many years after the event, Holmes recounts to Watson his life at university: 'You have never heard me talk of Victor Trevor? He was the only friend I made during the two years that I was at college. I was never a very sociable fellow, Watson, always rather fond of moping in my rooms . . . Trevor was the only man I knew, and that only through the accident of his bull-terrier freezing on to my ankle one morning as I went down to chapel'. First into the lists, in 1928, was Monsignor Ronald Knox in his seminal paper 'Studies in the Literature of Sherlock Holmes', published as one of his *Essays in Satire*. Quickly off the mark, he raises the point that the whole incident of Trevor's dog must be untrue: in neither university were dogs allowed within college gates. But going on to allude to Reginald Musgrave, the scion of a wealthy family and the only other acquaintance Holmes is known to have made while up, Mgr Knox, avoiding more exacting speculation, chooses Oxford. 'More and more', he writes, 'as I consider the wealth of his two friends, the exclusive aristocracy of the one, and the doggy tendencies of the other, together with the isolation which put even so bright a light as Holmes's under a bushel — more and more I incline to the opinion that he was up at the House [Christ Church].' He dares postulate even a college, when the university itself is in doubt!

Nothing daunted, T. S. Blakeney joins in the fray some four years later with his classic book *Sherlock Holmes — Fact or Fiction?*, and berates Mgr Knox for leaning towards Christ Church and Oxford. Trevor would have been far more likely to go to Cambridge, being a Norfolk man; add to that Holmes's bent for chemistry and the evidence is positively in favour of Cambridge. As for the terrier, says Mr Blakeney, we are not told that Holmes was within college gates anyway: he was on his way to chapel and was probably bitten in the town.

At this juncture, we see two points in the same *Gloria Scott* passage already quoted that need, and have received, close examination and interpretation. The episode of the bull-terrier, firstly, and then Holmes's use of the words 'during the two years that I was at college', are vital pieces of evidence, and when they are taken in conjunction with another statement by Holmes they become positively fraught. For, in *The Musgrave Ritual*, he speaks of 'my last years at the university'. These are deep waters, my dear Watson, for how to equate that with 'the two years that I was at college'?

Miss Dorothy L. Sayers attempted to do so in 1946 with her note on 'Holmes's College Career' in *Unpopular Opinions*. By dint of superbly thorough, though somewhat contorted, argument, she suggests that Watson misreported Holmes's actual words — that what he said was 'during the *first* two years at college' (my emphasis). She rejects what is perhaps the more likely error — that Holmes said '*in* college' (my emphasis) — because she has already decided that the university in question is Cambridge, and Cambridge men do not usually live in during their first two years. Thus Holmes was living out of college when he met Trevor and the dog; thus he was bitten in the street. Further evidence of a non-canine nature leads her to a partial identification of Sherlock as the T. S. Holmes who matriculated from Sidney Sussex in 1872.

Bernard Darwin, better known, perhaps, for his writings on golf, but an occasional commentator on matters Sherlockian, weighed in pleasantly two years later in his article 'Sherlockiana — The Faith of a Fundamentalist'. Though stating his basic conviction that everything occurred exactly as laid down in the stories, and lambasting those who probed further ('I do not wish to be uncharitable and so to condemn the commentators as very wicked people; I regard them merely as misguided, and all their daring and brilliancy slip off me as easily as water off a duck's back'), nevertheless he showed himself not immune to the disease and, agreeing with Miss Sayers about the dog and the university, suggested, however, that Magdalene and not Sidney Sussex was the college in question.

It is entirely fitting, therefore, that the Master of a Cambridge college should take up his pen and expatiate upon the matter. One might have expected him to rebuff Darwin and welcome so illustrious a former pupil as Holmes to Cambridge with open arms; but Sir Sydney Roberts, Master of Pembroke, was later to become President of The Sherlock Holmes Society of London and his 1953 rejection of Miss Sayers's theory was nothing if not scholarly. Adducing Max Beerbohm in his support, he suggested, in *Holmes and Watson — A Miscellany,* that perhaps Trevor's dog was chained up in the porch of the college, an Oxford custom alluded to in *Zuleika Dobson,* and that it was there that the incident took place, thus permitting Sherlock to be living in college at the time and thus in Oxford. Or, fully accepting the Sayers argument on living in and out of college at Oxford and Cambridge, Sir Sidney postulated that it was a Sunday service that Holmes was attending, that he merely stepped out into the street to buy a paper before going back into chapel, and was there, outside, brutally assaulted by the terrier. Slightly unfairly, Sir Sidney then proceeded to demolish the Sayers identification of T. S. Holmes and Sidney Sussex: that gentleman, he discovered, later became Chancellor of Wells Cathedral. Unfair, you see, because that is not really playing the game — the Sayers Sherlock-cricket game already alluded to.

At almost the same time, Gavin Brend was devoting a sizeable portion of his charming 1951 book *My Dear Holmes* to a discussion of the problem. While accepting Miss Sayers' theory as 'ingenious', Mr Brend nevertheless rejects it as implying that rules were always adhered to: 'Is this', he asks, 'quite the picture that one has of either Oxford or Cambridge? Could not the dog have been smuggled into the College for the purpose of some practical joke?' Or further, he suggests, might the terrier not have been hurt out in the street and run into the college in pain, to end by fastening on to Holmes? Other evidence leads Mr Brend to accept Oxford as having been Holmes's *alma mater.*

You see, then, the fundamental importance of that bull-terrier — how supporters of both camps use it to their advantage, contorting their arguments to show how it might have had the opportunity to attack the young Sherlock. A later commentator, Mr Percy Metcalfe, writing in *The Sherlock Holmes Journal,* suggested ingeniously that there are several colleges in both Oxford and Cambridge with parts of their buildings on either side of a road (easier, you see, for a dog purportedly not allowed in college grounds to assault Sherlock). For those of the Oxonian faction, this immediately brings to mind, among other possibilities, University College, with a part of the college separated from the remainder by the narrow width of Logic Lane.

But far more persuasive argument on behalf of Univ. had come already in 1958, when Roger Lancelyn Green, by dint of reading the *Dictionary of National Biography,* proved that University College at least, at the beginning of the 1870s, *did* permit dogs within its bounds. This was the bombshell that caused (or should have done so, were not Sherlockian studies so perennially fascinating and enjoyable) the Cambridge league to retire gracefully from the field, colours held high but acknowledging honourable defeat. In a letter to *The Sherlock Holmes Journal,* Mr Lancelyn Green quoted from the *D.N.B.* entry on George Granville Bradley, Master of Univ. from 1870: 'Bradley was determined to raise the standard of industry and insisted that every commoner should read for an honour school. Some consequent unpopularity was increased by an edict banishing dogs from the college, but he had his way . . .'. Thus dogs *were* permitted within Univ. bounds, and in fact we know the exact date on which Bradley laid down his

High Street, with University College and the entrance to Logic Lane on the left (note the dog in the bottom left-hand corner!). c. 1885.

edict: in his diary for Hilary Term 1871, Charles Cree, a Univ. undergraduate, noted on Saturday 11 March: 'Notice put up stating that "Dogs would be excluded entirely next term"; torn indignantly from the notice board and destroyed . . . When I had gone to bed great howlings were heard in quad demonstrative of the indignation felt by certain members of the College at the Notice concerning "Dogs".' Further evidence that Oxford colleges had permitted dogs to enter was adduced in 1970 when Lancelyn Green quoted a letter of 1875 from C. L. Dodgson (Lewis Carroll) to a lady who had been refused entry into Christ Church because of her dog: 'The general law about dogs, to which you were an unfortunate victim, is beneficent in its general action, as you would allow if you could have seen the College as I knew it years ago, with 70 dogs on the premises, day and night.'

Thus the central argument may be disposed of in Oxford's favour; but there are further nuggets of evidence on which the Oxonian may consolidate his position. *The Gloria Scott* and *The Musgrave Ritual* are the sole adventures in the Canon during which Holmes refers to his own university days; but on at least three other occasions during his career he visited Oxford or Cambridge. Let us briefly examine each case and see how it bears on the general proposition.

In investigating the disappearance of *The Missing Three-Quarter* Holmes and Watson travelled to Cambridge: it is so stated in the story and is unassailable. How does Holmes speak of the place? 'And now, my poor Watson, here we are, stranded and friendless, in this inhospitable town.' Hardly, as many critics have pointed out, the devoted product of a Cambridge college referring to his old university. Mention elsewhere in the story of 'a friendly native' is conclusive neither way. Gavin Brend made a further telling, if abstruse, point militating against Holmes having attended Cambridge and thus knowing the surrounding area. In his search for the missing rugby player Godfrey Staunton, Holmes visits in turn some local villages: 'I have covered some ground: Chesterton, Histon, Waterbeach and Oakington have each been explored and have each proved disappointing.' An interesting route, mused Brend, in that the far more obvious order to visit, because of connecting roads, would have been Chesterton, Waterbeach, Histon and Oakington. '. . . the route actually taken', he comments, 'reveals the Oxonian in a hurry who has not yet had time to procure a map.'

In 1903 — or so the chronologists of the Sherlock Holmes cases would have us believe — Holmes and Watson went to 'Camford' to look into the strange business of *The Creeping Man,* the distinguished Professor Presbury who was seen to perform, for no apparent reason, such feats as shinning up the wisteria plant that grew on his house. 'Camford', obviously, is a veiled reference to Cambridge or Oxford, and as such we must look for any evidence of familiarity betrayed by Sherlock. Happily, for an Oxonian, the evidence is there in abundance. 'In the meantime', says Holmes, 'we can only . . . enjoy the amenities of this charming town' — a striking contrast to 'this inhospitable town' that we know to be Cambridge. Add to that two quotations which denote previous acquaintance with the place: 'There is, if I remember right, an inn called the Chequers, where the port used to be above mediocrity and the linen above reproach.' Then, when Holmes states boldly 'There is an early train to town, Watson', it surely implies casual familiarity with the timetable rather than hurriedly-garnered information from Bradshaw's. Once more we may compare this with Holmes's ignorance, in *The Missing Three-Quarter*, of the existence of a late train from London up to Cambridge — almost inconceivable if he had been an undergraduate at the latter.

A few years ago an attempt was made by Trevor H. Hall, in *Sherlock Holmes — Ten Literary Studies,* to identify the 'row of ancient colleges' mentioned by Watson in *The Creeping Man* as those to be seen in Cambridge along St John's Street, Trinity Street and King's Parade: in order, the cab would have swept past St John's, Trinity, Caius, Senate House, King's and St Catharine's. But two can play that game. Say that Holmes and Watson were in Oxford and on their way from the High Street (off which there still is a Chequers inn — more of this later) to North Oxford, where Presbury would undoubtedly have lived; what more obvious route, then, than the High, into Turl Street, turn right into the Broad and left into Parks Road? A veritable profusion of

colleges and university buildings rear up on the right-hand side: Lincoln, Exeter, the old Ashmolean Building, the Sheldonian Theatre, the Clarendon Building, a corner of Hertford, the Indian Institute, Wadham and the University Museum. Had Watson also been looking to his left, he would have seen Jesus, Balliol, Trinity and Keble. Finally, in the evidence provided by *The Creeping Man,* Presbury, we are told, was Professor of Comparative Anatomy at the University. In 1903 Oxford precisely had the Linacre Chair of Comparative Anatomy: Cambridge had the *double* Chair of Zoology and Comparative Anatomy. A small indication, but telling.

We end by investigating the locale of the adventure of *The Three Students,* that trio of unhappy undergraduates each suspected of having cheated by copying a passage for translation in the Fortescue Scholarship papers. Mgr Knox and Sir Sidney Roberts blithely point to this story as proof that Sherlock had been at Oxford, in that Holmes talks easily of 'quadrangle'. Ah, but had they examined their texts with a little more diligence, they would have discovered an abundance of differing references: certainly Holmes on one occasion speaks of a quadrangle — but three pages earlier he refers to a 'courtyard' (the Cambridge usage). Hilton Soames, lecturer and tutor at St Luke's, who had called on Holmes's services, also mentions a courtyard, while Watson causes total confusion by alluding to a 'court' *and* a 'quadrangle'. Betraying as it does Watson's unfamiliarity with the terms — only one, of course, is permissible at each university — neither faction may take any comfort here.

Much has been made of the single sentence spoken by Soames: 'You are aware, Mr Holmes, that our college doors are double'; on the basis of this assumed familiarity it has been taken by at least one scholar that Holmes was at St Luke's himself in his undergraduate days, and that therefore wherever *The Three Students* adventure took place was also Holmes's university. That is perhaps a rather hasty judgement, for it fails to take account of a further quotation

Part of the 'row of ancient colleges' mentioned in *The Creeping Man*: Turl Street, with Lincoln College in the foreground, and Exeter further along on the right — the shadows on the left are those of Jesus, and part of Trinity is visible at the top of the street. c. 1890.

from Watson's pen, that Hilton Soames was an acquaintance of some years' standing: they had '*always known* him to be restless in his manner' (my emphasis). If Soames were an acquaintance of the two men, then it is perfectly feasible that they had visited him before, and thus that Holmes would be aware of the nature of the St Luke's doors. There is no need, therefore, on the basis of that one sentence, to suppose that Holmes attended the university wherein the story occurs; and that is a happy thought for the Oxford camp. There is, you see, incontrovertible proof that this adventure took place in Cambridge.

This proof hinges on the small black balls of clay and sawdust which, discovered by Holmes both in Soames's rooms and at the university athletics grounds, led him to the identification of Gilchrist as the cheating miscreant. Gilchrist was a long-jumper and had been practising before he entered Soames's rooms, and the clay substance came from his jumping spikes. C. B. Fry, the great Oxford athlete and, later, journalist, recalled that in his university days the jumping pit was filled only with 'soft, sandy material', and as one who broke the world record in the long-jump while still an undergraduate, it is wise to believe him. On the other side, there is positive evidence that just such a clay substance was in use in Cambridge. In *The Baker Street Journal* in 1971, Jacques Barzun quoted a 1946 letter from George Lyttelton to the critic James Agate: '. . . in those days, whatever it may be now, it was only at Fenner's, Cambridge, where he could have jumped into black clay. The normal long-jump bed was of loose brown loam, but old Watts, the Fenner's groundsman, produced this stuff — probably from the fens — claiming (quite rightly) that, as there was no crumbling at the edges of a footprint, measurement of the jump was far more accurate. Surely this is proof positive.' It is now accepted as such: Gilchrist jumped in Cambridge; but that does not bother our basic thesis, the identification of Holmes's university, one jot.

Happy the senior university to accept him as its own. Even if all the foregoing has been too detailed and top-heavy with scholarship, we may end this section by adopting the delightfully breezy approach of Michael and Mollie Hardwick, who dealt with the problem in *The Sherlock*

Holmes Companion by asserting: '. . . we will merely plump for Oxford. In spirit we have encountered Holmes in the High; we have never yet so much as caught the flutter of his undergraduate's gown in Christ's Pieces.'

The College

The university, then, is decided upon. But the net must be drawn tighter and the answers must be more precise: which college did Sherlock Holmes attend at Oxford? Here, of course, the arguments cannot be so firmly based as those on the greater question of the university. Evidence pointing in any direction at all, let alone in different directions, is so thin on the ground as to be almost invisible, and it might be thought that any decision on the matter could only be achieved by the toss of a coin. Mgr Knox, of the Oxford faction, has suggested Christ Church; the dog edict and the public thoroughfare of Logic Lane might tend to persuade one of the virtues of University College . . . clearly in this area one cannot hope to do more than put forward evidence that may possibly appeal to, and convince, readers more than the purveyors of previous theories have managed to do.

I shall, then, briefly state my contention that Sherlock Holmes attended St John's College, Oxford, as an undergraduate, having come from Merchant Taylors' School shortly before his sixteenth birthday in 1869 (1854 is the generally accepted date for Holmes's birth) — prodigiously precocious, but not too surprising to those who have followed his later extraordinary career. He took his Finals in 1873, and went down three years later at an age when most men would be entering their third undergraduate year. By this time, he had taken his Master of Arts degree, but undergone a complete change of mind over what he wanted to do in life.

'Enough . . . enough! Give me evidence! Give me proof!' you mutter. I shall endeavour to do so.

The *Oxford University Calendar* is an invaluable volume. Every year for the last century and a half, a thick book is published by the university, giving the names of all men (and now women, of course) studying at Oxford that year, together with all the Fellows of the various colleges and halls; details are given of examination results, both preliminary and final; and, of course, the examination requirements for that year are published — the rubric of the several courses, saying what an undergraduate will or will not have to study if he wishes to obtain an honours degree in the subjects available. Using the *Calendars* as any interested Sherlockian might do, I opened the index of names for a representative year when Sherlock *must* have been up at university, and looked down the columns, seeking out the name 'Holmes'. There was only one, a certain Edmond Gore Alexander Holmes, whose dates were reasonable, and that proved to be the starting point. How pleasant it was to see all fitting so neatly into place, with little or no stretching of the bounds of credulity.

A general view of St Giles, with St John's visible between the trees in the middle distance, taken in 1878, only two years after Holmes left the college.

Mr E. G. A. Holmes went up to St John's College in 1869: let me quote the *Calendar* for 1870 on the awards available from that college:

> Under an Ordinance of the University Commissioners, amended by a Committee of the Privy Council, the foundation is hereafter to consist of . . . five open Scholarships and twenty-eight appropriated Scholarships tenable for seven or five years, by persons elected from Merchant Taylors' School who shall not have attained the age of nineteen, and from the other schools who shall not have attained the age of twenty at their election, viz. twenty-one to Merchant Taylors' School, two to Coventry, two to Bristol, two to Reading and one to Tunbridge. There is also one open Scholarship, called the Holmes Scholarship, tenable for four years, without limitation in regard to age.

How happily named a scholarship!

This Holmes is listed as receiving one of the Merchant Taylors' School Scholarships on the foundation of the college. Now this identification of Edmond Gore Alexander as Sherlock necessitates some small rethinking on our Holmes's education. Hitherto, it has been assumed that Holmes and brother Mycroft were attended by private tutors, the evidence for this being based primarily, so far as I can see, on there being no mention at all in the stories of normal schooling. Such negative evidence does not seem conclusive in any way to me, and certainly does not rule out the possibility of a normal public school education. Granted that Holmes would not be the typical product of such a school, nevertheless if his family was conservative enough to send him to one of the great ancient universities of tradition, then why not to the Merchant Taylors' School, founded by the Merchant Taylors' Company in 1561? It was a public day-school, thus affording the young boy an ideal opportunity to develop various interests other than learning, unbothered by the calls of 'Lights out!' and the ghastly uniformity of junior dormitories inevitable at boarding school. And who would not be proud to be associated with a school among whose other products have been the poet Edmund Spenser, Robert Clive ('Clive of India') and John Walter, founder of *The Times*?

Because of the close association between the school and St John's at Oxford, there must have been little doubt that the young and brilliant Holmes would proceed there, and we ought not to be overly surprised at his extreme youth on being elected to a scholarship. Young he was, certainly; but Oxford has never shrunk from giving genius its head, and in any case, being admitted to a university when most are still working their way through school is not so rare. In 1967 Dr Harvey Friedman gained an Assistant Professorship at Stanford, California, when he was nineteen — and he already had a Ph.D. The recent case of Miss Ruth Lawrence at Oxford is even more spectacular: she graduated in 1985, after only two years' study, with First Class Honours in mathematics, aged fifteen.

But back to St John's in 1869. The new undergraduate, presumably looked on with awe by the others of his year, settled in and started on his studies of Literae Humaniores, or Lit. Hum. I quote from the *University Calendar* for 1875, when E. G. A. Holmes's B.A. degree was announced:

> The *stated* subjects of examination are:—
>
> A. The Greek and Latin languages
>
> B. The histories of ancient Greece and Rome to be studied in the original authors (Candidates must show such knowledge of Classical Geography and Antiquities and of the General History of Greece and Rome, as well as of the History of Philosophy, or of the History of the periods of Philosophy to which the philosophical authors offered by them belong, as shall be necessary for the profitable study of the authors or periods which they take up)
>
> C. Logic and the Outlines of Moral and of Political Philosophy, at least two treatises thereon by ancient authors to be offered. The writings of modern Philosophers are admitted but not required.
>
> Under the head of Logic, Candidates are recommended to study the following subjects:— The nature and origin of knowledge; The relation of language to thought; The history of Logic in Greece to the time of Aristotle inclusive; The theory of the Syllogism; Scientific Method, including a comparison of the methods of different sciences, and the principles of historical evidence.

What, then, of chemistry? Surely that is what everyone has always thought Holmes studied? Studied, yes, but not necessarily for his undergraduate degree. His course is nowhere mentioned. The case of *The Gloria Scott* reveals that he did some experiments in organic chemistry, but that was during the long (summer) vacation, that is, specifically *not* during term-time at Oxford. I tend to look on this as Holmes's primary interest outside his university studies: to achieve a 'profound' knowledge of chemistry, as Watson once put it, he must have spent nearly all his time, apart from his formal university work, on research and experimentation.

The Literae Humaniores course, furthermore, was a very relevant course of study to assist in the development of the Sherlock Holmes whom we know later. It is quite clear that he had a solid grounding in the Classics. On separate occasions (find them for yourself in the stories), he mentions, or quotes knowledgeably, Horace, Tacitus and Euclid: he thought enough of Petrarch to own a pocket copy of his works. Obviously Holmes was at ease in both Latin and Greek. And what of his knowledge of philosophy? Well, there are too many examples of Holmes himself philosophising along classical lines for me to quote here, but the evidence is there in the four long and fifty-six short stories. Again, look at Part C. of the course he had to follow: Logic, involving both the history of Logic and the examination of the Scientific Method. Does it not seem likely that it was his study of Logic at Oxford that first set Sherlock Holmes on the path towards becoming one of the greatest ever exponents of logical induction and deduction?

As well, perhaps, to clear up one outstanding point from the last section at this juncture, the question of those 'two years at college'. To me, Holmes's words to Watson are crystal clear and most precise. Two years he spent in college and the remainder of his time at Oxford (the other two undergraduate years to complete the four-year Lit. Hum. course, and three more years to conclude the stipulated seven-year period of his scholarship from Merchant Taylors' and to qualify for his M.A.) was spent in lodgings elsewhere in the town. Thus we also have 'my last years at the university': a member of the university and, indeed, still on the foundation of St John's, but not *in* college.

What, now, of the 'slight acquaintance' Holmes had with Reginald Musgrave, that 'scion of one of the very oldest families in the country'? Victor Trevor was the closer friend, but Musgrave, we are told in *The Musgrave Ritual,* attended the same college as Holmes, and the two knew each other well enough for the wealthy young aristocrat to have no hesitation in consulting his erstwhile undergraduate contemporary some years later. Holmes took his Finals in Michaelmas Term 1873, and the *Calendar* for 1875 tells us that he was placed in Class I. Thus he was free, for three years, to study what he liked — and it will probably have been at this time that he switched his interests from the Classics to a full-time education in the Natural Sciences — and developed those powers first made evident in the Norfolk village of Donnithorpe when he aided Trevor in the affair of *The Gloria Scott*. Talk spread throughout the college and university, and among those who learned of the special talents of the young Holmes was Musgrave, who had come up to Oxford precisely in 1873, the start of Holmes's 'last years at the university'. Look once again in the *University Calendar*, this time for the year 1874, and there you will find mention of a certain George Musgrave coming up to St John's as a commoner of the college. This is too much for coincidence: we must surely identify George as Reginald! Musgrave took his B.A. in 1876, a fact indicating that he did not subscribe to the longer Lit. Hum. course (although I can find no mention anywhere in the relevant *Calendar* of the subject of Musgrave's degree, still less in what class the Public Examiners placed him). Four years later, when Holmes had taken rooms near the British Museum in London, in Montague Street, and Musgrave had inherited the Hurlstone estates and entered Parliament, the aristocrat came to consult the penurious investigator. That four-year gap is given in the canonical story, and the year we come up with, 1880, is attested to by at least one of the major chronologists of the cases of Sherlock Holmes, the American Jay Finlay Christ in *An Irregular Chronology of Sherlock Holmes of Baker Street*, published in 1947.

A brief paragraph now to identify another contemporary of the young Holmes while up at Oxford. You may remember that, while looking into the nefarious pursuits of Charles Augustus Milverton in the late '80s or '90s (depending on which of those scholarly chronologies you put your faith in), Holmes adopted the alias of 'Escott' when he was wooing and winning Milverton's housemaid Agatha. In passing, not that this should draw us from the central importance of his choice of name — to be explained in a moment — this incident involving Milverton's housemaid is surely an answer to all those who bay at Sherlock's misogynist pronouncements: when duty called (and this was the only way, Holmes decided, in which he would be able to get the information on the girl's despicable employer that he needed), the detective was as smooth an operator in matters amorous as anyone might envy. But remember 'Escott'. Holmes chose the guise of 'a plumber with a rising business' as a suitable concomitant to this assumed name, but it is most unlikely that the man whose name Holmes adopted followed that profession in real life. The ever-present *Calendar* shows, in 1873, that John Howard Sweet Escott had come up to St John's on an Open Scholarship the previous year. Certainly he must have made an impression on Sherlock for him to have remembered, and made use of, the name even fifteen years later, let alone twenty-five.

So there we have it: Holmes's life and friends at St John's, Oxford, in the early 1870s. Whether or not it was so for Sherlock himself, those times were certainly idyllic; in his

The gentlemen of St John's at archery practice — the beautiful grounds of their college a few years before Holmes came up to join them. 1862.

history of the college (*Oxford University College Histories — St John's,* 1898), W. H. Hutton quotes the following extract from a letter by H. W. Burrows, later Canon of Rochester:

> You have no idea how beautiful at present (April) our groves are: the horse-chestnuts are luxuriantly green, and their dense foliage is a beautiful contrast to the more backward trees, which have not yet flushed into variety along our dazzling white roadways; while the grass is so soft, and the flowers so sweet, and the college so abbey-like, the place so cool and so quiet, that I think, with a bell in the distance, dying and swelling, it unites as many conceivable delights as any spot since Paradise.

Holmes's Oxford

The Oxford that Sherlock Holmes knew in those now impossibly halcyon days of the 1870s differed only in details and social attitudes from the Oxford of today. While now you may walk down university thoroughfares unafraid that your status as an undergraduate may lead you into danger, in 1871 Charles Cree could mention almost as a throwaway line in his previously quoted diary: 'Monday 6 November . . . Jim managed to get into a "scrummage" with the "Town" in Brasenose Lane, and bore off marks of the battle on his countenance.' Confrontations between the two factions that, perforce, inhabited Oxford started centuries ago; and only now can one really say that overt hostility is a thing of the past. Lingering suspicions on both sides may still remain, but they express themselves today in terms of sarcastic comments rather than well-aimed kicks. Complaints there may be still about current undergraduates at Oxford and their habits: they arise, however, more out of twentieth-century economic problems, whereby a student on a state grant who is not eternally at his books in his rooms or in the Bodleian Library is automatically thought to be an intolerable burden on the taxpayer.

A hundred years ago, when Holmes was up at Oxford, friction and violence between Town and Gown were born out of mutual distrust and — from Town to Gown, at any rate — a measure of envy and fear through ignorance. At best, then, an uneasy harmony — at worst, nightly scuffles and brawls. In one sense, the boundary fences between the factions in Oxford then were not so marked as they have become since. The wit who spoke of Oxford being 'the Latin Quarter of Cowley' described the present in satirical terms, when William Morris's brainchild of cheap, mass-market cars has transformed the city socially and physically. Oxford was literally towed into the twentieth century on the bumper of a Morris car; yet the modern and traditional must live together, and the Regius Professor of History at the University, representing all that he does, jostles down the High Street shoulder to shoulder (if not arm in arm) with the Cowley shop steward.

In the 1870s, industry, as we understand it, had not really arrived in Oxford. It was a town of several private brewers; there was — and is yet — a papermill at Wolvercote; and the Bookbinders' Arms public house in Jericho tells its own story as a local watering-hole for those employed by the Clarendon Press. Otherwise, Oxford was an admixture of the normal Victorian spirit of commercial enterprise and a wistful hanging-on to things rural: agricultural tools were still sold in St Ebbe's Street and cattle came to market in what is now the bus station at Gloucester Green. While that open market was emphatically for the Town and Country group in Oxford, its counterpart — the Covered Market, hidden away up four alleys behind the frontage of High Street shops — which might be thought to be the very hub of Town merchants, was in fact officially run by the University. Today, the *University Gazette* still gravely catalogues the election of the Clerk to the Market — an honorary title, pure and simple, now — but John Betjeman, in his published collection of Victorian and Edwardian photographs of Oxford, has a marvellous study of the coming together of two cultures: we see the produce of one Mr Piggott (who stares proudly at the camera) being weighed by the venerable and begowned figure of the Provost of Worcester College, white beard flowing, to ensure that, in this part of the Market at least, no short measure is being given.

On one side of the High, Frank Cooper's grocery shop, at Nos 83-84, reigned supreme for both Town and Gown shoppers, and as 'Sole Manufacturers of The Oxford Marmalade'. Founded in 1840, it was a classic example of the local firm making gigantic strides forward, such that in 1874, while Sherlock Holmes was still up at the university, the family was able to open its marmalade factory at new premises, in Victoria Buildings, near the railway station. That was the new spirit of the age. But cross to the other side of the High, stroll through the historic setting of Radcliffe Square (in which it is possible to stand and see none but university buildings on every side) and you find yourself at the Sheldonian Theatre, where only a decade earlier undergraduates had yelled and bayed at Matthew Arnold as he delivered the 1864 Creweian Oration: 'Cut it short! Give him beer!' Is that not a scene that could have come from the very Middle Ages? What, too, was a modern Victorian member of the 'Town' to make of the promise which, for six hundred years, every Oxford graduate had to give, that he would never on any account be reconciled with a certain Henry, son of Simeon, who had murdered a scholar in 1242?

This is not to suggest that the university failed entirely to move with the times; but the gulf was wide and the university, well aware of the Victorian spirit — and itself producing some of the figures central to that spirit — tended to keep itself to itself and change later rather than earlier. Nearly two decades before Holmes went up to St John's, change had been very much in the air when, on 31 August 1850, a Commission was appointed to enquire into the state, discipline, studies and revenue of the University of Oxford. The Chairman was an august figure from the religious world, the new Bishop of Norwich — himself a former undergraduate at Queen's — and his brief, and that of his six colleagues on the Commission, was necessarily wide.

Prime among their targets was the level of wealth required to put a gentleman through four years at Oxford, and the consequent social aspects of being an undergraduate. There was a very general desire to extend the benefits of the university to a poorer class, a class (and we are not discussing the poor as such, but rather the merchant and commercial classes) dissuaded from sending their sons to Oxford because of the high cost involved. As an example, the Commissioners noted that a student at a Hall in Durham could live on sixty pounds a year; on the other hand, the figure of seven hundred and twenty-five pounds quoted as the expenses of a Commoner at Worcester College over four years was stated in evidence to the Commission as being low for an Oxford man.

The gathering of evidence in this and all other relevant fields was, as may be imagined, immensely difficult and time-consuming, the Commissioners being able to report only in April 1852; and a further two years were needed before an Act of reform was passed through Parliament, reconstituting the government of the University and generally ushering in such an era of change that Oxford was revolutionised, albeit quietly. As C. E. Mallet commented in his *History of the University of Oxford* (1927): 'Vested interests, obsolete regulations, encumbering restraints were swept aside, and endowments too long indifferently applied were made available for wider use.' It is, however, instructive to note the tone of the objections that had been expressed by opponents of the reformers while the Commission was still at work. The evidence of Frederick Temple, later headmaster of Rugby and Archbishop of Canterbury, must have been typical of that given by those who thought the overall proposals went too far and changed too much: 'It is frightful to think of the large proportion of the undergraduates who are tainting their minds, not unfrequently for life, with the effects of an unpure youth. To prevent this altogether would be doubtless impossible; but the difference between rendering vice easy or hard of access is immense. It is a duty to protect the weak by putting barriers in the way to evil. This plan would throw all barriers down.'

So the Oxford that Sherlock Holmes discovered in 1869, and the university he knew for seven years, was no longer the other-worldly community it had been earlier in the century. The need for change had been accepted and reforms had been achieved. This is not to say, of course, that the old ways and attitudes died — far from it. Maybe Oscar Wilde was as untypical as an undergraduate as he was a law unto himself after his university days; but a bill is extant from G. H.

Osmond, the jeweller and silversmith of St Aldate's, which shows typical objects on which he chose to spend his money while up at Magdalen College. Dated towards the end of 1876, it shows purchases of a set of 18-carat gold studs at two guineas, a gold collar stud at 15/- and an ivory stud at a mere shilling. As a footnote to these purchases, it is interesting to note that Wilde failed to pay the bill and was taken to the Chancellor's Court by Mr Osmond. History does not record the eventual outcome of this very Oxford case.

While the young Holmes is unlikely to have been as gaudy as Wilde, one can clearly see that the tastes evident in his later life were fostered at Oxford. One hopes that, owing to his extreme youth, he had not yet taken up pipe-smoking by his first year, but it is pleasant to imagine Holmes, nearly eighteen and at the end of his two years of living in college, watching his scout (servant) laying the coals of his early morning fire, and perusing the breakfast menu while drawing meditatively on a pipe newly-acquired from Messrs J. Mayo & Son of the Cornmarket — whence, in 1875, he could have purchased a carved meerschaum pipe for £3 17s. Mayo's also advertised themselves as 'Importers of Wines, Spirits and Cigars'; the Sherlock Holmes who, many years later, was able to provide 'a group of ancient and cobwebby bottles' at the close of the affair of *The Noble Bachelor*, must have owed to his Oxford years an education in matters of wine as well as his education in matters more formally cerebral. More convenient than Mayo's for Holmes will have been E. Workman's (later E. F. Greenwood's) of 73 St Giles's, directly opposite St John's College. Or he could have consulted the list of D. Eaton's at their establishment below the Town Hall, specialising in such exotica as 'East India Madeira', 'Cape Wines' and 'Muscat of Rivesaltes' alongside more conventional clarets, Burgundies, Hocks and Moselles. For more convivial occasions, when drinking in the town was preferable to drinking on college premises (always remembering that he had to be back in St John's by nine o'clock in the evening, or risk capture by the Proctors and their university police, the Bulldogs), Holmes will have attended the Chequers inn, off High Street, later to be so fondly remembered for its port and linen; the landlord at that time was one E. Gardener, Esq., according to *Shrimpton's Oxford Directory* for 1875.

Charles Cree notes in his diary a day spent with friends near the Perch inn, during which a certain 'Holmes' (no further name is given) was the cause of some merriment. This was very much the age of the 'College man', when the Oxford undergraduate looked no further than the confines of his own college for most of his academic, sporting and social life. Yet it does not stretch the bounds of credulity too much to picture Cree, at Univ., learning of the youthful prodigy Sherlock Holmes — who, by his own later admission, was 'always rather fond of moping in [his] rooms . . .' — and dragging him out with a circle of high-spirited young gentlemen for some sport at the ancient inn.

It is, by and large, a happy and tranquil picture we have, both of the Oxford of the 1870s and of the young Sherlock Holmes who was part of that university for seven years. While appearing much of the time to be a loner who mixed little with men of his year — almost certainly feeling himself at a disadvantage, thrown so young into so heady an atmosphere — nevertheless, if we have been correct in our surmises, he never had any but the happiest memories of his time up at Oxford. His later Bohemianism, tastes both high- and low-brow, attitudes to the law and pompous authority, and political and spiritual beliefs — all these can be traced back to the formative years at Oxford. It is unusual, perhaps, for a product of Oxford University in the 1870s to speak in such hopeful and positive terms of the Board schools many years later; but the man who could discourse so eloquently and beautifully on the theme of a rose, and the consequent existence of a beneficent Providence (Holmes discusses both the Divinity and the schools during the course of *The Naval Treaty*) undoubtedly bears the marks of an intellect moulded in part by the religious foundation that is St John's College, Oxford.

Postscript 1985

I should like to think that the original publication of *Sherlock Holmes at Oxford* in 1977 had put an end to all scholarly speculation about Holmes's university and college. Almost, but not quite! Only two important further contributions to the subject have appeared since then, although this is doubtless attributable to the constant flow of material on every conceivable facet of the lives and behaviour of the Baker Street duo; specific topics sometimes take a back seat for years.

But in the March 1979 issue of *The Baker Street Journal*, Robert A. Moss made the novel suggestion that Holmes read chemistry at Christ Church, Oxford, *under an alias*, and then moved on to Cambridge. No proof is adduced for the alias theory, alas, but the author's reasoning for Christ Church is sound.

'Every indication we have from the Canon indicates that, once resolved to read chemistry, Holmes would seek out the best college in which to read, and the best tutor with whom to study,' says Moss, and he points out that Augustus Vernon Harcourt, assistant to the Aldrichian Professor of Chemistry, Sir Benjamin Brodie, was a Reader at Christ Church. Brodie was succeeded in 1872 (the year he proposes for Holmes's matriculation) by someone less interested in practical chemical research, and this led to Holmes leaving Oxford without a degree and moving on to Cambridge.

The other new article is by Bernard Davies, long-time Holmesian scholar, in *The Sherlock Holmes Journal* for Summer 1985; by dint of careful research into the adventure of *The Gloria Scott*, he concludes that the case took place in either 1873 or 1874. A study of Oxford and Cambridge dates for their long vacations (summer holidays) in each year leads inexorably — I am glad to say — to another conclusion: that Holmes and the young Trevor *must* have been at Oxford.

So, the latter piece only adds credence to my own ideas; the former is too glib an example of the two-university theory — is it perhaps too easy an option, an ideal way in which to wriggle out of the central problem? Despite Mr Moss's gentle criticism that 'the scanning of mouldering University Calendars and Honours Lists may well be futile', I remain faithful to Mr Edmund Gore Alexander Holmes of St John's College, Oxford.

Bibliography

Works of Sherlock Holmes scholarship consulted include:

Essays in Satire by Ronald Knox, Sheed and Ward 1928

Sherlock Holmes — Fact or Fiction? by T. S. Blakeney, John Murray 1932

Unpopular Opinions by Dorothy L. Sayers, Victor Gollancz 1946

An Irregular Chronology of Sherlock Holmes by Jay Finlay Christ, privately printed 1947

Every Idle Dream by Bernard Darwin, Collins 1948

My Dear Holmes — A Study in Sherlock by Gavin Brend, George Allen & Unwin 1951

Holmes and Watson — A Miscellany by S. C. Roberts, Oxford University Press 1953

The Sherlock Holmes Companion by Michael and Mollie Hardwick, John Murray 1962

Sherlock Holmes — Ten Literary Studies by Trevor H. Hall, Gerald Duckworth & Co. 1969

Also articles and correspondence in *The Sherlock Holmes Journal* and *The Baker Street Journal.*